CHAMOMILE

meow

TROUBLE

Katherine Battersby

VIKING

Our new neighbor
turned up one day
without warning.

I don't know where
he came from, but I knew
just by looking at him . . .

He was TROUBLE.

Chamomile and I had seen his type before.
We could hear him through our shared wall.

He was a wild animal.

He had terrible teeth.

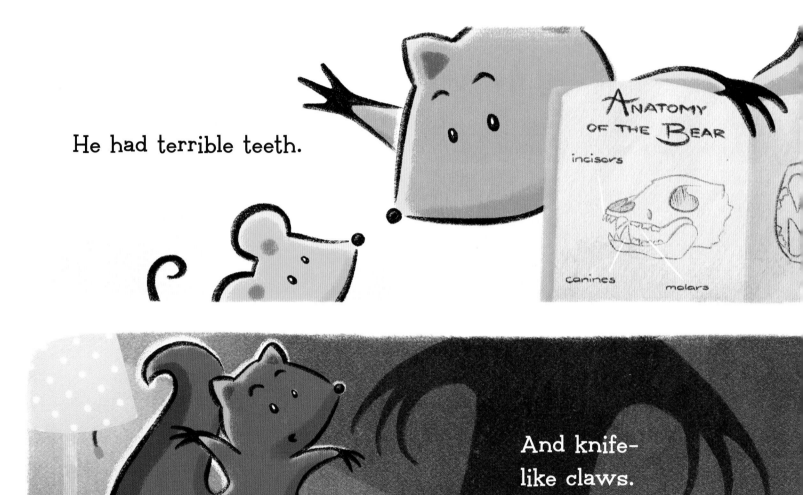

ANATOMY
OF THE BEAR

incisors

canines   molars

And knife-
like claws.

And huge,
horrifying
hungers.

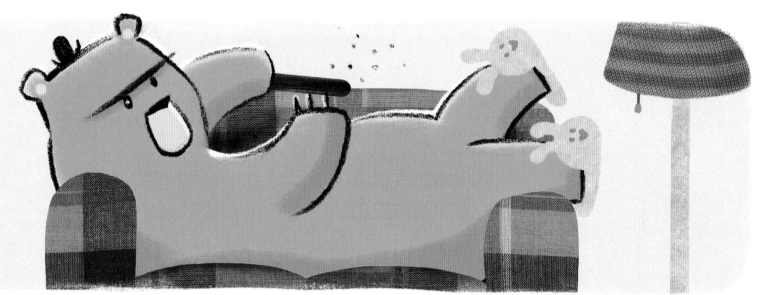

Trouble was NOT
to be trusted.

Trouble wore strange clothes
and did strange things.

I just ignored him.

But it wasn't long before
Trouble came knocking.

I knew he was
up to no good.

Trouble lurked around every corner.

That's when something
horrible happened . . .

TROUBLE
ATTACKED!

Now I was the wild animal.

I had to protect Chamomile.

But Trouble followed close behind.

Nowhere was safe.

So I stacked up
and packed up—

and was ready to
leave for good, but . . .

Where was
Chamomile?

Next door,
TROUBLE was
up to something
suspicious.

Then I heard . . .

TROUBLE had Chamomile! He was going to *eat* her.

He would gnash his terrible teeth . . .

and slash his knifelike claws . . .

and fill his huge, horrifying hunger!

I burst in, ready
for TROUBLE.

meow?

And that's when
I realized . . .

he wasn't Trouble.

I was.

I wanted to say sorry,
but I didn't know how.

So instead I said,
"Do you drink tea?"

Well, it turns out
that tea and cookies
are the perfect pair.

Each may be different . . .

But somehow they
make the other better . . .

and suddenly you can't
imagine life any other way.

For Susan–
a friendship formed over tea and cookies

VIKING

An imprint of Penguin Random House LLC, New York

First published in the United States of America by Viking, an imprint of Penguin Random House LLC, 2021

Copyright © 2021 by Katherine Nicole Battersby

Visit us online at penguinrandomhouse.com.

LIBRARY OF CONGRESS CATALOGING-IN-PUBLICATION DATA IS AVAILABLE.

ISBN 9780593114049

Manufactured in China   Set in Plumbsky Black   Book design by Katherine Battersby and Jim Hoover

The illustrations for this book were rendered in pencil, collage, photography, and digital media.

1   3   5   7   9   10   8   6   4   2

ONTARIO ARTS COUNCIL
CONSEIL DES ARTS DE L'ONTARIO
an Ontario government agency
un organisme du gouvernement de l'Ontario